This book belongs to

_____

The
Bremen Town
Musicians

BY

The Brothers Grimm

Retold by Samantha Easton

ILLUSTRATED BY

Mark Corcoran

ARIEL BOOKS

ANDREWS AND McMEEL
KANSAS CITY

Library of Congress Cataloging-in-Publication Data

Easton, Samantha.
    The Bremen town musicians / the Brothers Grimm ; retold by Samantha Easton ; illustrated by Mark Corcoran.
       p.   cm.
    Summary: Four animal friends who are no longer wanted by their masters set out to become musicians in the town of Bremen, but along the way encounter a den of thieves.
    ISBN 0–8362–4925–9 : $6.95
    [1. Fairy tales. 2. Folklore—Germany.] I. Corcoran, Mark, ill.
II. Bremer Stadtmusikanten. III.Title.
PZ8.E135Br   1991
398.2—dc20   91–2910
[E]   CIP
                                           AC

Design: Susan Hood and Mike Hortens
Art Direction: Armand Eisen, Mike Hortens, and Julie Phillips
Art Production: Lynn Wine
Production: Julie Miller and Lisa Shadid

The
Bremen Town
Musicians

Once there lived a donkey who had worked many long years for his master.

One day the donkey overheard his master say, "That old donkey of mine is no good for anything. He can't even carry the sacks of grain to the mill any more. I'm just going to have to get rid of that bag of bones some-how!"

When the donkey heard that, he decided he had better run away. He liked music very much and had heard that Bremen was a very musical town. So he thought he would go there and become a town musician.

The donkey had not gone very far when he came upon an old dog. The dog was lying panting in the middle of the road.

"Hello there, Old Hound," said the donkey. "Why are you lying there out of breath?"

"Oh," sighed the dog, "because I am old and weak. I'm not much good at hunting any more, so my master decided to get rid of me. I got wise to his plans and ran away, but now I don't know what to do!"

"Don't let that get you down," said the donkey. "Why don't you come with me? I'm going to Bremen to be a town musician. We could team up. I'll play the guitar and you can play the drums. How about it?"

"That sounds fine to me!" said the dog.

So he and the donkey continued on
together. After a time they came upon an
old cat.

She was sitting by the side of the road
sighing. "What's the matter, Whiskers?"
asked the donkey. "You look as if you've for-
gotten how to smile!"

"I don't have much to smile about,"
sniffed the cat. "I'm getting on in years. My
teeth aren't as sharp as they once were, and
I'm not as fast as I used to be. These days I'd
rather sit by the fire and sleep than run

around and catch mice. My mistress threatened to drown me, but I escaped just in time. But now I don't know how I'll earn my milk!"

"Don't worry about that," said the donkey. "Why don't you join us? We're on our way to Bremen to be town musicians. I know you have a great voice, and we'd be happy to have you come with us. What do you say?"

"It sounds like a good idea!" said the cat. So she joined the donkey and dog on the road to Bremen.

Soon the three friends came to a farm-yard. A cock sat on the gate, crowing at the top of his lungs.

"What's on your mind, Old Red Comb?" called the donkey. "You're raising such a racket, you're making my ears hurt!"

"I'm sorry about that," said the cock. "It's only that . . . well . . . I learned today that my mistress is having company tomorrow and she wants to cook me in a stew! Since tomorrow morning my head will be chopped off, I want to crow while I still can!"

"That doesn't sound good!" said the donkey. "Why don't you come with us instead? We're on our way to Bremen to be town musicians. We could certainly use a singer like you. I just know that if we all played together, we'd come up with some great tunes. Will you join us?"

"I think I will!" said the cock.

The four friends continued on the road to Bremen. But the town was too far away to reach in a single day. As the sun was setting, they found themselves at the edge of a forest.

"Oh, dear," said the donkey. "We better look for a place to stay. I hope we find a place where I can get a bite to eat and a bed of straw."

"And I hope we find a place where I can get a bone or two to gnaw on," said the dog.

"I hope we find some place warm!" said the cat.

"I'd like a place that has some corn to peck and a roof to roost on," said the cock. "Perhaps I'll fly to that treetop and look around."

So the cock flew to the top of the tree and looked north, south, east, and west.

Soon he came flying down. "There's a light over there," he reported, pointing with his claw. "I think it's a house!"

"That sounds good to me," said the donkey. "Let's go!"

So the four animals set out in the direction of the light. Soon they came to a house with all its lights blazing.

As he was the tallest, the donkey trotted up and peered through the window.

"What do you see, Donkey?" the others asked.

"Hmmm," said the donkey. "We've come to a house full of robbers, that's clear. I can see them inside sitting around a table and stuffing themselves with food!"

"Really?" said the dog. His ears pricked up at the mention of food, for he was very hungry.

"Yes," replied the donkey. "How I wish we could get inside!"

"We must come up with a plan," said the cat.

"Yes, indeed," agreed the cock.

So the four friends thought and thought,

and finally the donkey had an idea. He laid his front hooves on the windowsill. The old dog jumped on his back, the cat climbed up on the dog's back, and the cock flew up and perched on the cat's head. When they were all in place, the donkey gave a signal and the four animals began making music together.

And what music it was!

The donkey brayed and the dog howled. The cat meowed and the cock crowed. They made their music as loudly as they possibly could while the donkey rattled the window with his hooves. The robbers jumped up in terror from the table.

"What is it!" shrieked one.

"A monster," screamed a second. "Listen to the noise it makes!"

"Perhaps it's a ghost!" yelled a third.

"Oh, no!" they all cried. Then the robbers ran into the woods, and they didn't stop to look back once!

After the robbers had gone, the four friends went into the house. They sat right down at the table and ate all the food that was left. They ate and ate until they were full. Then the donkey began to yawn.

"I don't know about the rest of you," he said, "but I think I'm going to find myself a nice bed!"

"Me, too," said the dog.

"I could use a snooze myself!" purred the cat.

"So could I," said the cock.

So they all went off to find a comfortable place to sleep. The donkey went into the yard and stretched out on a pile of straw. The dog flopped down behind the door. The cat curled up in front of the fire. The cock flew up to the roof to roost. Within moments, all four friends were fast asleep.

Some time later the robbers noticed that the lights in the house were out and everything was quiet.

"We should never have run away so quickly," grumbled the chief robber. He ordered one of his men to steal back to the house and see whether anyone was there.

The robber was afraid, but he couldn't say no to his chief.

When the robber reached the house, he found it dark and silent. So he tiptoed into the kitchen to get a light from the fireplace. He mistook the glowing eyes of the cat for live coals and leaned down to light a match from them. But the cat was in no mood for such games. With a hiss, she leaped at the man's face and scratched him!

"Ouch!" the robber screamed and he ran for the back door. There he stumbled over the dog who jumped up and bit him in the leg!

"Help! Help!" cried the terrified robber and he ran out the door and dashed across the yard. There, he bumped into the pile of straw and woke up the donkey.

"What's this?" the donkey thought and gave the robber a hard kick. That woke up the cock, who crowed from the rooftop with all his might, "Cock-a-doodle-do!"

At this the robber ran back to his chief as fast as he could.

"That house is terrible!" he chattered, trembling all over. "There's a mean witch in the kitchen! She hissed at me and almost scratched out my eyes with her fingernails! Behind the door, there's a man with a knife. Look, he stabbed me in the leg! Out in the yard there's a monster with an iron club, and he beat me black and blue! And on the roof, there sits a judge who looked at me and cried, 'Hang that robber at once!' I managed to escape this time, but I'll never ever go back!"

When the robbers heard that they decided never to go near the house again!

But the four Bremen town musicians de-cided they liked the house very much.

"Why should we go somewhere else," said the donkey, "when we can make beautiful music right here?"

The dog and the cat and the cock agreed. So the four friends stayed on in the robbers' house and they were very happy. Indeed, for all I know, they are still there!